Las piezas del puzle

Para Lady Sarah Maclean

Las piezas del puzle

Babette Cole

SerreS

Malas noticias
en los periódicos.

Guerras en
la televisión.

Cosas extrañas

en la
calle.

Ziggi canta…
Le encanta la música.
Tiene una canción para
cada momento.

¿Tiene sentido?

"¿Qué hago yo aquí? ¿Por qué he nacido?",
suspiraba Ziggi.

"¿Y si cantas sobre eso?",
le preguntó Albert.

La noche era muy oscura y las
estrellas brillaban sobre la ciudad.

Ziggi y Albert observaban el cielo y cantaban
a las estrellas su nueva y triste canción.

¡Y ocurrió algo maravilloso!
Una de ellas les escuchó…
¡Y cambió el rumbo!

¡Algo resplandeció ante ellos!
Y no era una estrella.
¡Pues claro que no!
Era un pequeño caballo alado.
Un caballo al que
también le gustaba cantar.

"Sujétate fuerte", cantaba el poni.
"Este será el mejor viaje de tu vida.
¡Ahora vas a entenderlo!"

"Mira ahí abajo… ¿Quiénes son?"

"Son mamá y papá", contestó Ziggi.

"Ellos nacieron para
que tú pudieras venir
al mundo", dijo el caballo.

"Los médicos,
las enfermeras
y los dentistas…
todos ellos nacieron
para que tú fueras
un niño sano."

"También tus maestros y profesores... ellos nacieron para ayudarte a cumplir tus sueños. De vez en cuando se enfadan, sí, pero debes escucharles cuando hablan."

"Deezee Jones, tu héroe, lo hizo.

Y nació para que tú
pudieras inspirarte en él."

"Algún día serás tan genial como él, ¿sabes?"

"Y aquí está la hermosa Bella.
Habéis nacido para amaros el uno al otro...
Y el cura... ¡el cura ha nacido para casaros!"

"Éstos son todos tus hijos.
Han nacido para ser tu futuro."

"Todo tiene sentido, porque todos tenemos un propósito en el mundo. Formamos parte de un gran puzle, en el que todas las piezas se necesitan y se apoyan en las otras. Así nos ayudamos."

"No importa quiénes somos ni de dónde venimos, todos hemos nacido y estamos aquí para trabajar unidos. Igual que en la música: ¡se necesitan un montón de notas para que suene la melodía perfecta!

Cuidar y compartir. Eso es
lo que hace girar al mundo."

"Pero, y *yo*... ¿Por qué he nacido *yo*?", preguntó Ziggi.

"¿Para qué estoy aquí?"

"¿Para qué? ¡Pues para decirles a todos lo que has visto!", contestó el pequeño caballo.

"Canta al mundo entero tu nueva canción, Ziggi."

"El sentido de la vida está en la vida misma.
Todos debemos trabajar
para hacer un mundo mejor.
Para querer y cuidar de los demás…
¡Para eso hemos nacido!"
"¡Por eso estamos aquí!"

… ¡Para eso hemos nacido!

Título original: *That's Why!*
Publicado por acuerdo con Random House
© del texto y las ilustraciones, Babette Cole, 2006
© de la traducción, Anna Duesa, 2007

© de esta edición, RBA Libros, S.A., 2007
Santa Perpètua, 12-14. 08012 Barcelona
Teléfono: 93 217 00 88 Fax: 93 217 11 74
www.rbalibros.com / rba-libros@rba.es

Primera edición: junio de 2007

Realización editorial: Bonalletra Alcompas, S.L.
Diagramación: Editor Service, S.L.

Referencia: SLHE067
ISBN: 978-84-7871-937-2

Hello, Mr. Dodo!

Nicholas John Frith

ARTHUR A. LEVINE BOOKS
AN IMPRINT OF SCHOLASTIC INC.

Martha was *cuckoo* about birds.

She knew every bird in the woods
behind her house.

"Hello,
Mr. Blackbird!"

"Hello,
Mr. Woodpecker!"

"Morning, Mrs. Sparrow!"

But one day, Martha spotted someone new.

She'd never seen a bird like this before. It was really funny-looking.

And big too.
The biggest bird that
Martha had ever seen.

"Hello,
Mr. Whoever-You-Are!"
she said.

The bird was a little shy at first,
but it soon took a shine to her.

It was very funny and friendly.

"But I still don't know what you are,"
said Martha. "I think I'll have to
look you up in my books."

It was a dodo — and it was supposed to be *extinct*!

Once there had been thousands of them, then they all disappeared. People had hunted them and eaten them for dinner.

No one had seen a dodo for hundreds of years.

DODO
(Raphus cucullatus)
EXTINCT

This was also the fate of the Moa bird of New Zealand. Many species of Moa once roamed the forests of New Zealand, some of them growing to more than three meters in height.

However, by the mid-1400s the Moa were all gone. They had been hunted to extinction when the Maori people arrived in New Zealand from Polynesia.

ther
FLIGHTLESS BIRDS
MOA

Dodos are not the only flightless birds to have become extinct after the arrival of human settlers.

The dodo has become a powerful symbol of endangered species.

The first recorded mention of the dodo was by Dutch sailors in 1598. It is thought that the hungry sailors hunted the bird to extinction not long after.

The fact that dodos were unable to fly, and had never been hunted before, made them particularly easy to catch.

The last sighting of a dodo was in 1662.

Records suggest that, before then, many dodos were transported to Europe, Asia, and elsewhere. It is not known whether any of the birds survived these long journeys.

Extinction of the dodo was not formally accepted until the 19th century.

An extinct flightless bird unique to Mauritius, an island to the southeast of the African continent.

Much about the dodo bird is unknown.

They were believed to have lived in wooded areas of the coast of the island. They grew to one meter in height, laid one egg at a time, and had a diet consisting mainly of soft fruits and seeds.

Mauritius 1648

"Poor things," thought Martha.
"Well, they're not going to eat *my* dodo."
And she decided to keep him a secret.

That summer, Martha learned a lot about dodos.

They were *terrible* at playing snap.

They *really* couldn't fly.

They *loved* doughnuts.

And they made the best friends *ever*.

All this time, Martha kept the dodo a secret.

Then, one afternoon . . .

. . . the secret just slipped out.

"Where are you off to with all those doughnuts?" asked the postman. "They're for my dodo," said Martha. "Dodos *love* doughnuts."

Oh, no!

What had she said? Now the
postman might tell everyone in
town. What would happen to Mr. Dodo
if people found him? She had to warn him — fast!

"Quick!" said Martha.
 "You've got to hide!"

But the dodo just wanted doughnuts.

"I can't visit you anymore," said Martha.
 "They might see me."

"Good-bye, Mr. Dodo," she sighed.
"Let's hope the postman doesn't tell anyone about you."

Unfortunately, he did.

The next day, a huge crowd gathered outside Martha's door. They were from the television, the newspapers, and the zoo. They were all shouting:

"Where's the dodo, Martha?"

What could Martha say?

So she said . . .

"He's right here!

"Can't you see him? Hello, Mr. Dodo!
Would you like a doughnut?"

"He's an *imaginary* dodo?" said the postman.
"But, of course," said Martha. "Dodos are extinct.
Everyone knows that!"

The crowd was very grumpy as they packed up and left.
But would it ever be safe for Martha to go and see the dodo again?
What if somebody spotted her?

As summer turned
to autumn . . .

. . . and autumn to winter,
Martha thought about
her friend.

She began to wonder whether she really had imagined him after all.

When spring came, she decided she had to go back and see.
She took some doughnuts with her, just in case.

She looked in all their
favorite places,

but she couldn't see him.

Then she held up her bag
of doughnuts, and shook it.
"Doughnuts, Mr. Dodo!"
she whispered.

There was a rustle in
the bushes behind her . . .

. . . and there he was!
"Mr. Dodo!" cried Martha.
"You're safe!"

And it seemed he'd been keeping
a secret of his own. There was
another dodo with him . . .

. . . and an egg!

BIRD SPOTTING
know your birds

1.

2.

3.

4.

5.

6.

7.

Other:

NAME: Martha

1. blackbird ☐
2. gull ☐
3. pigeon ☑
4. oystercatcher ☑
5. sparrow ☑
6. magpie ☑
7. woodpecker ☑

Other: dodo

For Mum and Dad, just because

Library of Congress Cataloging-in-Publication Data available

ISBN 978-1-338-08939-4

10 9 8 7 6 5 4 3 2 1   17 18 19 20 21

Printed in Malaysia 108
First American edition, February 2017